FIRE TRUCK TO THE RESCUE!

By Sonia Sander
Illustrated by MADA Design

SCHOLASTIC INC.

NEW YORK   TORONTO   LONDON   AUCKLAND   SYDNEY

MEXICO CITY   NEW DELHI   HONG KONG   BUENOS AIRES

ISBN-13: 978-0-545-11543-8
ISBN-10: 0-545-11543-4

LEGO, the LEGO logo, the Brick and Knob configurations and the Minifigure are trademarks of the LEGO Group. ©2009 the LEGO Group. All rights reserved. Published by Scholastic Inc. SCHOLASTIC and associated logos are trademarks and/or registered trademarks of Scholastic Inc. Manufactured by Scholastic Inc. under license from The LEGO Group.

12 11 10 9 8 7 6 5 4 3 2 1   40   17/0

Book designed by Cheung Tai & Henry Ng
Printed in the U.S.A.
First printing, April 2009

Oh no!
Smoke is in the air.
There is a fire in the city.

Call 911 right away!
The firefighters can save the day.

5

B-r-r-r-i-i-n-g!
The fire alarm rings.
The firefighters are on their way.

One by one, they jump into action.
They slide down the pole.

The firefighters dress in a flash. They grab their hats and boots.

V-r-o-o-o-m! V-r-o-o-o-m!
The fire truck is ready to go.

W-o-o-o-o! Honk! Honk!
The fire truck races down the road.

21

Meow! Meow!
Up goes the ladder. One brave firefighter saves the cat.

Look high up in the sky.
Here comes even more help.

At last the fire is out.
The tired firefighters head home.

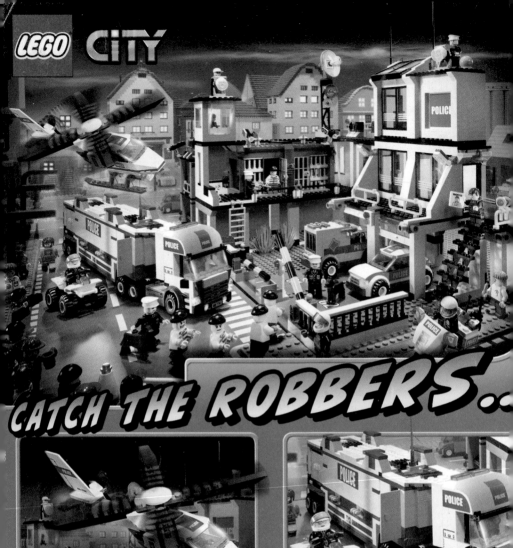

LEGO CITY

CATCH THE ROBBERS...

...WITH THE LEGO® CITY POLICE COLLECTI
- Catch the robbers with the police truck
- Take them to the police station
- Lock them up in the prison block